WITHDRAWN
Hotchkiss Public Library
P.O. Box 540   JAN 07
Hotchkiss, CO 81419

RECORD
BREAKERS

Jim Winchester

GARETH**STEVENS**
PUBLISHING
A Member of the WRC Media Family of Companies

Please visit our web site at: **www.garethstevens.com**
For a free color catalog describing Gareth Stevens Publishing's
list of high-quality books and multimedia programs,
call 1-800-542-2595 (USA) or 1-800-387-3178 (Canada).
Gareth Stevens Publishing's fax: (414) 332-3567.

Library of Congress Cataloging-in-Publication Data

Winchester, Jim.
    Record breakers / by Jim Winchester.
        p. cm. — (Aircraft of the world)
    Includes bibliographical references and index.
    ISBN-10: 0-8368-6905-2 — ISBN-13: 978-0-8368-6905-7 (lib. bdg.)
    1. Aeronautics—Records—Juvenile literature. I. Title. II. Series.
    TL537.W56   2006
    629.1309—dc22   2006004070

This North American edition first published in 2007 by
Gareth Stevens Publishing
A Member of the WRC Media Family of Companies
330 West Olive Street, Suite 100
Milwaukee, WI 53212 USA

Original edition copyright © 2006 by Amber Books Ltd
Illustrations and photographs copyright ©
International Masters Publishers AB/Aerospace–Art-Tech

Produced by Amber Books Ltd., Bradley's Close,
74–77 White Lion Street, London N1 9PF, U.K.

Project Editor: Michael Spilling
Design: Brian Rust

Gareth Stevens editor: Carol Ryback
Gareth Stevens art direction: Tammy West
Gareth Stevens cover design: Scott M. Krall
Gareth Stevens production: Jessica Morris

Measurements appear in statute miles.

All rights reserved. No part of this book may be reproduced, stored
in a retrieval system, or transmitted in any form or by any means,
electronic, mechanical, photocopying, recording, or otherwise,
without the prior written permission of the copyright holder.

Printed in the United States of America

1 2 3 4 5 6 7 8 9 10 09 08 07 06

Cover and title page: Amelia Earhart chose to
fly the Lockheed Vega to set many of her speed,
altitude, and endurance records.

Contents

Words that appear in the glossary are printed in **boldface** type
the first time they occur in the text.

Wright "Flyer"

- First powered flight in history
- Home-built aircraft

After years of experiments with models, kites, and gliders, brothers Orville and Wilbur Wright built the world's first successful motor-powered airplane, the "Flyer."

Although they came from Dayton, Ohio, the brothers tested their designs at Kitty Hawk, on the North Carolina coast. In that area, steady winds blow inland

The Wright "Flyer" was the world's first true airplane. Its short flying life proved that manned, powered flight was possible.

from the Atlantic Ocean. Those strong winds helped the Wright craft fly properly, and the remote location kept away competitors and nosey reporters.

On December 17, 1903, Orville Wright made the first flight in

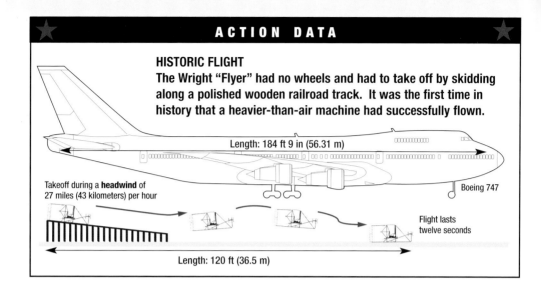

ACTION DATA

HISTORIC FLIGHT
The Wright "Flyer" had no wheels and had to take off by skidding along a polished wooden railroad track. It was the first time in history that a heavier-than-air machine had successfully flown.

Length: 184 ft 9 in (56.31 m)

Boeing 747

Takeoff during a **headwind** of 27 miles (43 kilometers) per hour

Flight lasts twelve seconds

Length: 120 ft (36.5 m)

the "Flyer." His journey lasted twelve seconds and covered only 120 feet (36.5 meters), a distance much shorter than the length of a modern Boeing 747 airliner.

That day, both of the Wright brothers took turns flying the plane, making a total of four flights. The longest lasted for nearly one minute and traveled 852 feet (260 m). Today, the Wright "Flyer" is on display at the National Air and Space Museum in Washington, D.C.

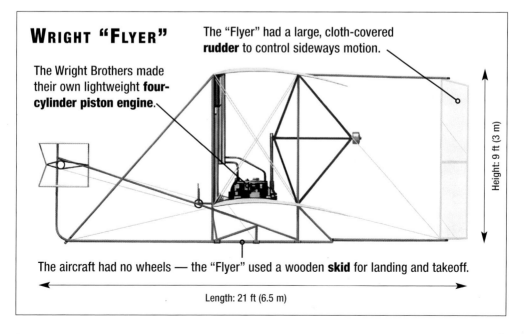

WRIGHT "FLYER"

The "Flyer" had a large, cloth-covered **rudder** to control sideways motion.

The Wright Brothers made their own lightweight **four-cylinder piston engine**.

Height: 9 ft (3 m)

The aircraft had no wheels — the "Flyer" used a wooden **skid** for landing and takeoff.

Length: 21 ft (6.5 m)

Blériot XI Monoplane

- First airplane to cross the English Channel
- Pioneering monoplane

Frenchman Louis Blériot was one of the first airplane builders to make a **monoplane** design. His Blériot XI airplane also had wheels rather than skids and a moveable **tailplane** and **fin** for control. Most modern airplanes also have these features, although they look very different. Having proved that his design could fly for long distances over land, Louis Blériot wanted to

Louis Blériot became one of the first international air travelers when he flew from France to England in 1909.

prove airplanes could fly between countries separated by water.

On July 25, 1909, Blériot took off from a field near Calais, France, heading northwest for Dover, England, on the opposite side of the English Channel. Another pilot, Hubert Latham,

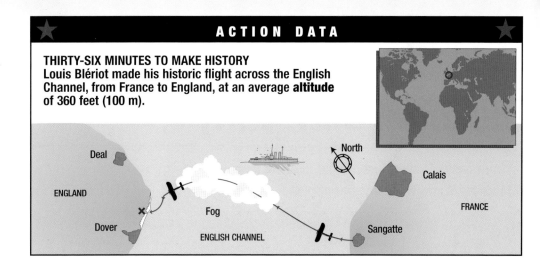

ACTION DATA

THIRTY-SIX MINUTES TO MAKE HISTORY
Louis Blériot made his historic flight across the English Channel, from France to England, at an average **altitude** of 360 feet (100 m).

Deal

North

Calais

ENGLAND

FRANCE

Fog

Dover

Sangatte

ENGLISH CHANNEL

also attempted the crossing that morning but crash-landed in the water and was rescued.

Bumpy Landing

Halfway across, Blériot nearly lost his way in heavy fog. After a flight of thirty-six minutes, he made a bumpy landing in a small valley near Dover Castle, which is on the southeast coast of England. Blériot won a large prize from a newspaper for being the first person to fly over the English Channel, and he became one of the most famous men of his day.

Within four years, Blériot's company had sold more than eight hundred similar airplanes in France, Britain, and Italy.

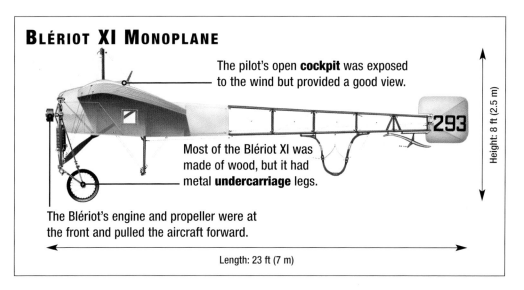

BLÉRIOT XI MONOPLANE

The pilot's open **cockpit** was exposed to the wind but provided a good view.

293

Height: 8 ft (2.5 m)

Most of the Blériot XI was made of wood, but it had metal **undercarriage** legs.

The Blériot's engine and propeller were at the front and pulled the aircraft forward.

Length: 23 ft (7 m)

Vickers FB.27 Vimy

- First nonstop transatlantic flight by Alcock and Brown
- Modified World War I bomber airplane

The Vickers Vimy was one of the largest aircraft in the world in 1919. A British team chose the Vimy for its first attempt at crossing the Atlantic Ocean by air. Several other airplanes had crashed trying to make the first air journey between North America and Europe.

A specially modified Vimy with extra fuel tanks was shipped to Newfoundland, Canada, in crates

Alcock and Brown's flight across the Atlantic marked the beginning of air travel between Europe and North America.

and reassembled in a field there. John Alcock and Arthur Whitten Brown set off from St. John's, Newfoundland, on the dangerous flight in their heavy, slow airplane on June 14, 1919.

Although it was summer, they flew into strong winds and then fog.

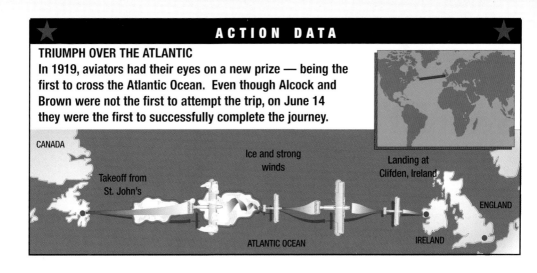

TRIUMPH OVER THE ATLANTIC
In 1919, aviators had their eyes on a new prize — being the first to cross the Atlantic Ocean. Even though Alcock and Brown were not the first to attempt the trip, on June 14 they were the first to successfully complete the journey.

CANADA

Takeoff from
St. John's

Ice and strong
winds

Landing at
Clifden, Ireland

ENGLAND

IRELAND

ATLANTIC OCEAN

Ice formed on the plane's wings. Brown had to lean out of the cockpit to chip away some of the ice. Later, they lost control but regained it just above the water.

They flew all night and arrived over the coast of Ireland at nine in the morning, after a flight lasting more than sixteen hours. Most of the flight took place at low altitude.

Seeing some flat ground near Clifden in County Galway, Ireland, they put the big aircraft down. The ground was very soft and the Vimy tipped on its nose. Despite the damage, it was repaired and put on display in London's Science Museum, where it still is today. Alcock and Brown became national heroes.

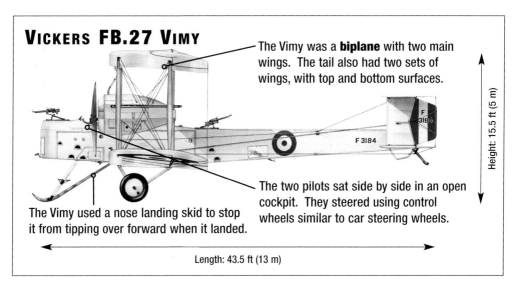

VICKERS FB.27 VIMY

The Vimy was a **biplane** with two main wings. The tail also had two sets of wings, with top and bottom surfaces.

Height: 15.5 ft (5 m)

F 3184

The Vimy used a nose landing skid to stop it from tipping over forward when it landed.

The two pilots sat side by side in an open cockpit. They steered using control wheels similar to car steering wheels.

Length: 43.5 ft (13 m)

Ryan NYP — *Spirit of St. Louis*

- First solo, nonstop transatlantic flight
- Early long-range monoplane

In the 1920s, pilot Charles Lindbergh became famous for his many flying skills. He also flew the first airmail route between St. Louis, Missouri, and Chicago, Illinois, in the mid-1920s.

During that time, Lindbergh learned of a contest with a $25,000 prize for the first transatlantic solo flight between the United States and mainland Europe. Lindbergh teamed up with some **investors** to build a plane just for the contest.

Lindbergh's historic transatlantic flight was not the first crossing ever, but it was the very first by a solo pilot.

The Ryan Company in San Diego, California, built a special version of a small airplane called the M-2 for Lindbergh's flight. Lindbergh named the new plane model the Ryan NYP — the initials stood for New York–Paris. That specific aircraft was named the *Spirit of St. Louis* in honor of the investors.

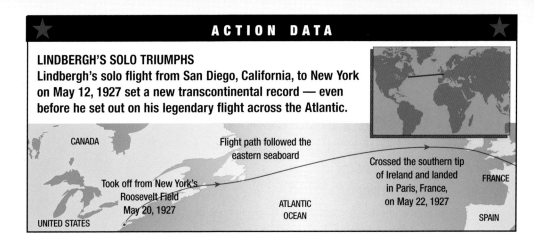

LINDBERGH'S SOLO TRIUMPHS
Lindbergh's solo flight from San Diego, California, to New York on May 12, 1927 set a new transcontinental record — even before he set out on his legendary flight across the Atlantic.

CANADA

Flight path followed the eastern seaboard

Took off from New York's Roosevelt Field May 20, 1927

Crossed the southern tip of Ireland and landed in Paris, France, on May 22, 1927

FRANCE

ATLANTIC OCEAN

UNITED STATES

SPAIN

Flying Fuel Tank

The NYP was basically a flying fuel tank. The entire front part of the plane contained fuel. Lindbergh did not have a front window. He could only see where he was going by sticking his head out a side window. On May 20, 1927, he took off from New York, carrying only sandwiches and some water. He landed at France's Le Bourget Airport near Paris thirty-three hours and thirty minutes later. Thousands of people greeted him. As the first pilot to fly solo across the Atlantic Ocean, Lindbergh became one of the most famous people in the world at the time.

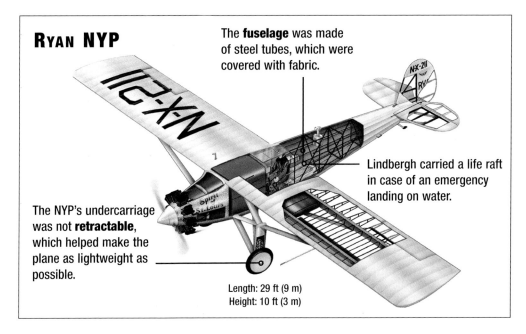

RYAN NYP

The **fuselage** was made of steel tubes, which were covered with fabric.

Lindbergh carried a life raft in case of an emergency landing on water.

The NYP's undercarriage was not **retractable**, which helped make the plane as lightweight as possible.

Length: 29 ft (9 m)
Height: 10 ft (3 m)

Supermarine S.6B

- **Fastest floatplane of its time**
- **Schneider Trophy winner**

In 1911, French businessman and hot-air balloonist Jacques Schneider decided to offer a prize for progress in flying.

Two years later, in 1913, the first Schneider Trophy went to the country with the fastest seaplane to complete a 150-mile (241-km) triangular flight course. France won the first Schneider Trophy.

The Schneider Trophy inspired designers in several countries to build better and faster airplanes in the 1920s and 1930s.

Its plane had a top speed of 46 miles (74 km) per hour. Britain won the 1914 Trophy. The race was not held again until 1919.

In those days, airfields had short runways that were too small for large aircraft. Seaplanes, which took off from water, were used for racing.

The Supermarines

In the 1920s, the United States, Britain, and Italy all won the Schneider Trophy at least once. The British company Supermarine won in 1922, 1925, and 1927, competing against the Italian Macchi planes. Reginald Mitchell, who later designed the Spitfire fighter plane, also designed the Supermarines.

The last and best of the racing planes was the Supermarine S.6B, which had a narrow fuselage and a thin wing. The engine's radiator was inside the wing, and the cockpit was very shallow, which helped reduce **drag** and increase speed — although the design gave the pilot a poor view.

In 1931, Britain's S.6B won with a speed of 340 miles (547 km) per hour. It was the last Schneider Trophy race, and Britain kept the trophy for good.

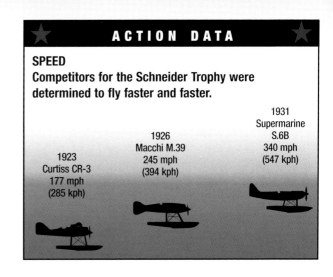

ACTION DATA

SPEED
Competitors for the Schneider Trophy were determined to fly faster and faster.

1923
Curtiss CR-3
177 mph
(285 kph)

1926
Macchi M.39
245 mph
(394 kph)

1931
Supermarine
S.6B
340 mph
(547 kph)

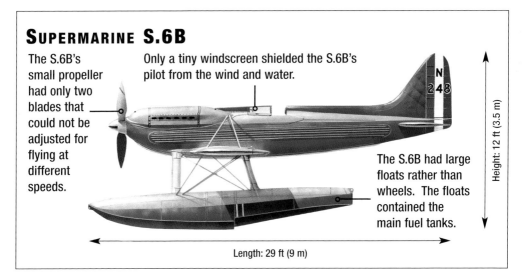

SUPERMARINE S.6B

The S.6B's small propeller had only two blades that could not be adjusted for flying at different speeds.

Only a tiny windscreen shielded the S.6B's pilot from the wind and water.

The S.6B had large floats rather than wheels. The floats contained the main fuel tanks.

N 248

Height: 12 ft (3.5 m)

Length: 29 ft (9 m)

Lockheed Vega

- First woman to cross the Atlantic Ocean on a solo flight
- Pioneering high-speed cabin monoplane

I n 1928, when Amelia Earhart became the first female to fly across the Atlantic Ocean, she was a passenger, not a pilot. But Earhart, like Charles Lindbergh, also hoped to someday make a transatlantic solo flight. She chose the Lockheed Vega, one of the most modern airplanes of the time, for her journey.

Earhart's solo flight began at Harbor Grace in Newfoundland,

Amelia Earhart used Lockheed Vegas on most of her many record-breaking flights.

Canada, on May 20, 1932. She ran into strong winds and icy conditions during the crossing. The Vega also had mechanical problems — the **altimeter** in the cockpit broke and a fuel tank began leaking.

Earhart planned to fly all the way to Paris, just as Lindbergh

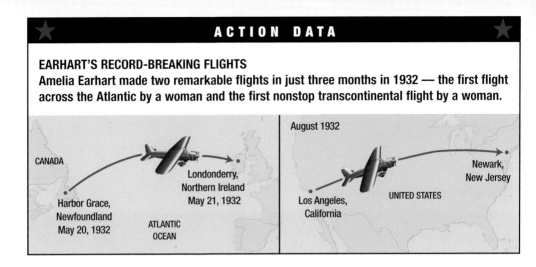

EARHART'S RECORD-BREAKING FLIGHTS
Amelia Earhart made two remarkable flights in just three months in 1932 — the first flight across the Atlantic by a woman and the first nonstop transcontinental flight by a woman.

CANADA

Londonderry,
Northern Ireland
May 21, 1932

Harbor Grace,
Newfoundland
May 20, 1932

ATLANTIC
OCEAN

August 1932

Newark,
New Jersey

Los Angeles,
California

UNITED STATES

had, but after thirteen hours and twenty-eight minutes, she landed near Londonderry, Northern Ireland. Earhart received medals from both the U.S. and French governments for her achievement.

Disappearance Over the Pacific

Also in 1932, Earhart was the first woman to fly nonstop across the United States. In 1935, she flew solo from Hawaii to Los Angeles.

In 1937, Earhart and her navigator, Fred Noonan, attempted to break the record for flying around the world. Their twin-engine Lockheed Electra disappeared somewhere over the Pacific Ocean in July 1937. They were never found.

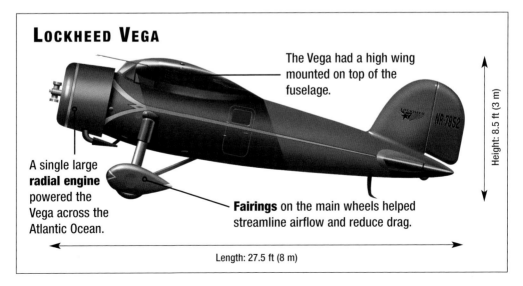

LOCKHEED VEGA

The Vega had a high wing mounted on top of the fuselage.

A single large **radial engine** powered the Vega across the Atlantic Ocean.

Fairings on the main wheels helped streamline airflow and reduce drag.

Height: 8.5 ft (3 m)

Length: 27.5 ft (8 m)

Bell X-1

- First aircraft to break the sound barrier
- Experimental rocket airplane

Jet airplanes could not reach supersonic speed — a speed faster than the speed of sound. As a jet increases its speed, its body shape **compresses** the air directly in front of the plane, preventing it from breaking the sound barrier.

The Bell X-1 was the first experimental aircraft to attempt supersonic flight.

The Bell X-1 test aircraft was specially built to fly at supersonic speeds. Its bullet-shaped, bright orange fuselage was easy to see from a great distance. Although the X-1 could take off on its own, a converted B-29 bomber usually carried it into the air.

Sonic Boom

Several test pilots flew the X-1, but the most famous was Charles E. "Chuck" Yeager. On October 14, 1947, his X-1, named "Glamorous Glennis" after his wife, dropped from the B-29 to fly free over the California desert. Yeager fired his rockets, and the X-1 roared away. With only a minute's supply of fuel, he climbed to 43,000 feet (13,000 m). Yeager flew the Bell X-1 just above the speed of sound, known as **Mach 1**.

Observers at Edwards Air Force Base below heard a **sonic boom** as Yeager's X-1 broke the sound barrier. Once the fuel ran out, the plane glided back down to Earth.

A sonic boom is so loud that it shakes the walls and can shatter windows in structures below.

ACTION DATA

SPEED OF SOUND
Chuck Yeager broke Mach 1 — the sound barrier — for the first time on October 14, 1947.

The B-29 climbed 23,000 feet (7,000 m).

The X-1 dropped away. Yeager waited until he was clear of the B-29 before firing all four rockets.

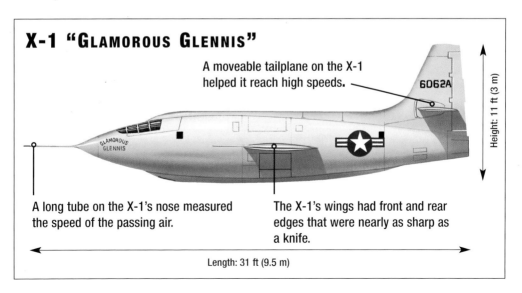

X-1 "GLAMOROUS GLENNIS"

A moveable tailplane on the X-1 helped it reach high speeds.

6062A

Height: 11 ft (3 m)

GLAMOROUS GLENNIS

A long tube on the X-1's nose measured the speed of the passing air.

The X-1's wings had front and rear edges that were nearly as sharp as a knife.

Length: 31 ft (9.5 m)

1967

North American X-15

- Fastest aircraft in history
- The world's highest flyer

In the late 1950s, North American Aviation built two X-15 rocket planes for **NASA**. The X-15s traveled at faster speeds and higher altitudes than any aircraft ever before. A B-52 carried the X-15 under its wing up

NASA used data from the X-15 test flights in the 1960s to design the space shuttle.

to launch altitude. After launch, the X-15 climbed to the edge of the **stratosphere**. Several flights went higher than 50 miles (80 km).

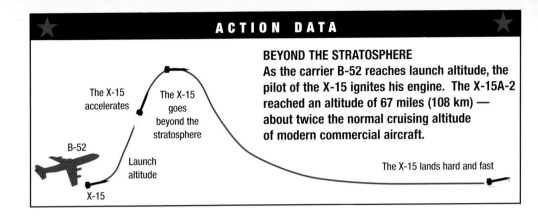

The X-15 accelerates

The X-15 goes beyond the stratosphere

B-52

Launch altitude

X-15

BEYOND THE STRATOSPHERE
As the carrier B-52 reaches launch altitude, the pilot of the X-15 ignites his engine. The X-15A-2 reached an altitude of 67 miles (108 km) — about twice the normal cruising altitude of modern commercial aircraft.

The X-15 lands hard and fast

NASA says the stratosphere is where Earth's atmosphere ends and space begins. Pilots who flew that high were considered astronauts. Neil Armstrong, the first astronaut to walk on the Moon, was one of the twelve X-15 test pilots.

Explosive Power

One X-15 exploded on the ground. The cockpit and other parts that suffered no damage were used to help build a larger version called the X-15A-2. In 1963, it reached the highest speeds of any manned aircraft until the space shuttle flew.

On October 3, 1967, X-15A-2 pilot Bill Knight reached 4,520 miles (7,300 km) per hour (Mach 6.72) — nearly seven times the speed of sound.

The X-15A-2's altitude record of 67 miles (108 km) lasted until 2004, when SpaceshipOne reached 71.5 miles (115 km).

X-15A-2

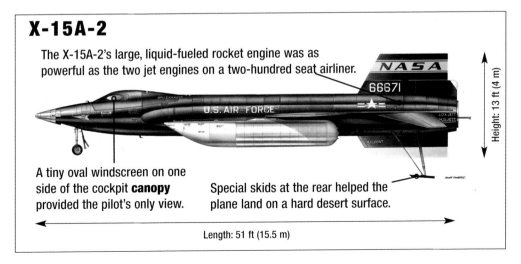

The X-15A-2's large, liquid-fueled rocket engine was as powerful as the two jet engines on a two-hundred seat airliner.

A tiny oval windscreen on one side of the cockpit **canopy** provided the pilot's only view.

Special skids at the rear helped the plane land on a hard desert surface.

Height: 13 ft (4 m)

Length: 51 ft (15.5 m)

Tupolev Tu-144

- First supersonic passenger transport
- Pioneer of supersonic technology

In the 1960s, several countries began developing a supersonic commercial airliner. Britain and France developed the Concorde. In the U.S., Boeing planned the 2707, but abandoned it before production began. The former Soviet Union was determined to fly the world's

The Tu-144's drooping nose gave pilots a good view during takeoff and landing.

first supersonic airliner and spied on its competitors. As a result, the **prototype** Tupolev Tu-144 flew on New Year's Eve 1968, two months before the Concorde. It looked a lot like the Concorde, though there

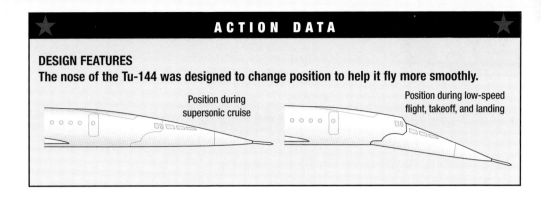

DESIGN FEATURES
The nose of the Tu-144 was designed to change position to help it fly more smoothly.

Position during
supersonic cruise

Position during low-speed
flight, takeoff, and landing

were many differences. The Tu-144 carried more passengers and flew faster. It was the world's fastest-ever passenger aircraft, and flew at Mach 2.25, more than two times the speed of sound.

Crash in Paris

One of the first Tu-144s crashed at the Paris Air Show in 1973. After that, the design was changed and later models had a different wing and bigger engines.

The Tu-144 began operations with the Soviet national airline Aeroflot in 1975. At first, it delivered mail from Moscow to the southern reaches of the country. Later it also carried passengers. Unfortunately, the Tu-144 broke down often. It was expensive to operate. Only sixteen were ever built. Aeroflot stopped flying the Tu-144 in the early 1980s.

In 1996, some U.S. companies and NASA bought a Tu-144 from the Russian Federation space agency. They used it to gather **data** to help with the design of new supersonic aircraft.

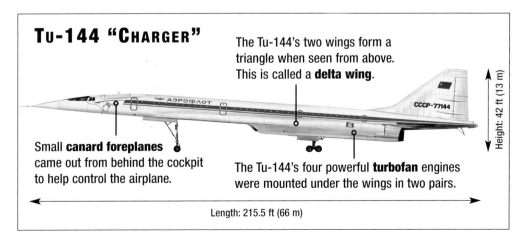

Tu-144 "Charger"

The Tu-144's two wings form a triangle when seen from above. This is called a **delta wing**.

Height: 42 ft (13 m)

Small **canard foreplanes** came out from behind the cockpit to help control the airplane.

The Tu-144's four powerful **turbofan** engines were mounted under the wings in two pairs.

Length: 215.5 ft (66 m)

Gossamer Albatross

- Pedal-powered flight across the English Channel
- Most succesful human-powered aircraft in history

California physicist Paul MacCready built the most successful human-powered aircraft ever made. His aircraft designs used pedal power and were much like bicycles with wings.

In 1979, MacCready's plane, the *Gossamer Albatross*, became the first human-powered aircraft to fly across the English Channel.

The *Albatross* was made of light materials. Without its pilot,

The *Gossamer Albatross* was the first human-powered airplane to fly over the English Channel.

the *Albatross* weighed only 70 pounds (32 kilograms). The pilot needed to be extremely fit and could weigh — at most — 150 pounds (68 kg). In order to keep the aircraft in flight and moving forward, the pilot had to pedal constantly at full power. Bryan

Allen, the man chosen to fly the *Albatross* across the English Channel, was a professional cyclist. He trained to pedal for long periods of time.

Crossing the Channel

On June 12, 1979 — almost seventy years since Blériot's first cross-channel flight — Allen left Folkestone on the southern English coast and started pedaling the *Albatross*. The plane had a wingspan of almost 95 feet (29 m).

Allen flew at a low altitude across the channel, never flying higher than 50 feet (15 m) above the water. After two hours and forty-nine minutes of hard work, he landed the *Albatross* at Cap Gris-Nez, France.

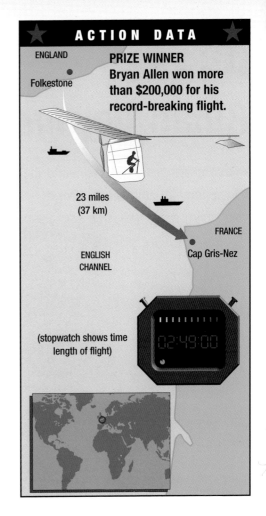

ACTION DATA

ENGLAND

Folkestone

PRIZE WINNER
Bryan Allen won more than $200,000 for his record-breaking flight.

23 miles (37 km)

FRANCE

Cap Gris-Nez

ENGLISH CHANNEL

(stopwatch shows time length of flight)

02:49:00

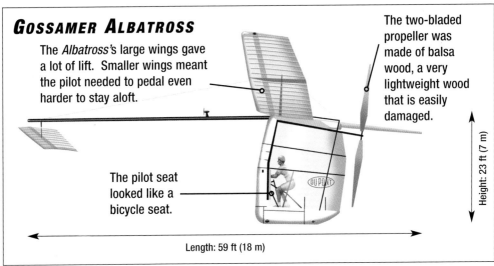

GOSSAMER ALBATROSS

The *Albatross*'s large wings gave a lot of lift. Smaller wings meant the pilot needed to pedal even harder to stay aloft.

The two-bladed propeller was made of balsa wood, a very lightweight wood that is easily damaged.

The pilot seat looked like a bicycle seat.

Height: 23 ft (7 m)

Length: 59 ft (18 m)

Rutan *Voyager*

- First nonstop, around-the-world flight
- Experimental long-range aircraft

T he Scaled Composites *Voyager* was an extraordinary airplane. It was built to make only one special flight, to fly around the world without landing or refueling in the air. Burt Rutan, who has designed many unusual airplanes, spent two years building the *Voyager* in Mojave, California.

***Voyager*'s wings were made of fiberglass and graphite — two lightweight materials — to save weight.**

Voyager had extremely long wings, which are good for long-range flight. Burt's brother, Dick, and Dick's girlfriend, Jeana Yeager, piloted *Voyager*. Their flight began on December 14, 1986 at Edwards

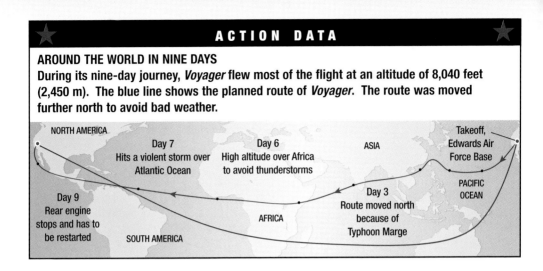

AROUND THE WORLD IN NINE DAYS
During its nine-day journey, *Voyager* flew most of the flight at an altitude of 8,040 feet (2,450 m). The blue line shows the planned route of *Voyager*. The route was moved further north to avoid bad weather.

NORTH AMERICA

Takeoff, Edwards Air Force Base

Day 7
Hits a violent storm over Atlantic Ocean

Day 6
High altitude over Africa to avoid thunderstorms

ASIA

PACIFIC OCEAN

Day 9
Rear engine stops and has to be restarted

AFRICA

SOUTH AMERICA

Day 3
Route moved north because of Typhoon Marge

Air Force Base, California. *Voyager*'s wings held the fuel and drooped down at the tips. During takeoff, the wingtips scraped along the runway and were damaged, but the crew decided it was safe to continue.

Avoiding the Hurricane

Voyager flew slowly, at about 116 miles (187 km) per hour.

Voyager had to fly around a hurricane. It also had to avoid flying over certain countries. Most of the time, it used only the rear engine to save fuel. During the flight, one pilot rested while the other flew. *Voyager* circled Earth before arriving back in California on the morning of December 23. The trip took nine days, three minutes, and forty-four seconds.

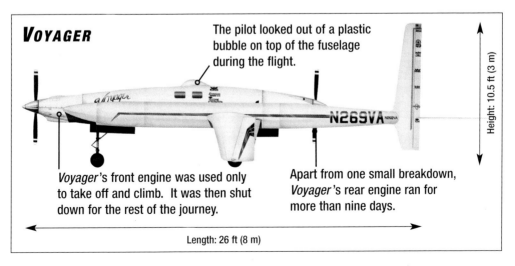

VOYAGER

The pilot looked out of a plastic bubble on top of the fuselage during the flight.

N269VA

Height: 10.5 ft (3 m)

Voyager's front engine was used only to take off and climb. It was then shut down for the rest of the journey.

Apart from one small breakdown, *Voyager*'s rear engine ran for more than nine days.

Length: 26 ft (8 m)

Antonov An-225 *Mriya*

- World's biggest aircraft
- Space shuttle carrier

The world's biggest aircraft is the Antonov An-225, which first flew in 1988. Its Russian name is *Mriya*, meaning "dream." The An-225 is made in Ukraine by Antonov, a company with a long history of building large aircraft. To make the An-225, Antonov took the world's biggest jet at the time, the An-124 freighter, added extra fuselage

The An-225 was brought out of retirement to perform heavy-lifting work all over the world.

sections, lengthened the wing, and gave it two more engines and a double tail. The Y-shaped double tail gave the airplane extra stability for carrying heavy loads. It also has seven pairs of wheels on each side instead of five.

The An-225 was built to carry the Soviet *Buran* ("Snowstorm") space shuttle between its launch and landing sites. The *Buran* flew in space only once, and the An-225 was put into storage. It seemed as if the An-225 might never fly again.

Return to Service

In 2000, the An-225 returned to service as a commercial freighter. It is popular with companies that move huge objects, such as oil-drilling equipment and disaster-relief supplies. Cargo is loaded through doors at the front of the aircraft. The An-225 can carry a load of 551,000 pounds (250,000 kg) and

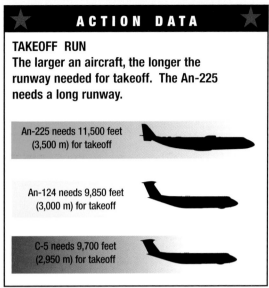

ACTION DATA

TAKEOFF RUN
The larger an aircraft, the longer the runway needed for takeoff. The An-225 needs a long runway.

An-225 needs 11,500 feet (3,500 m) for takeoff

An-124 needs 9,850 feet (3,000 m) for takeoff

C-5 needs 9,700 feet (2,950 m) for takeoff

is the world's heaviest aircraft. Only the "Spruce Goose" flying boat had longer wings. Only one *Mriya* has been completed. A second aircraft is slowly being finished using money earned by the first one. A third An-225 may be built someday.

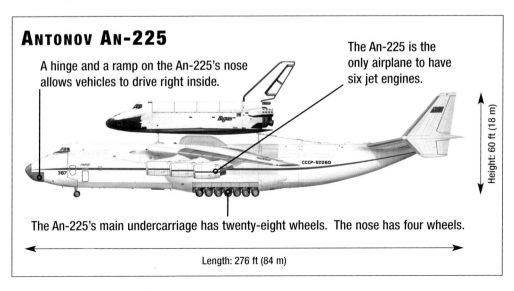

ANTONOV AN-225

A hinge and a ramp on the An-225's nose allows vehicles to drive right inside.

The An-225 is the only airplane to have six jet engines.

Height: 60 ft (18 m)

The An-225's main undercarriage has twenty-eight wheels. The nose has four wheels.

Length: 276 ft (84 m)

Airbus A380 Superjumbo

- **World's largest commercial passenger aircraft**
- **New breed of superjumbo passenger airliner**

The Airbus A380 is the world's largest commercial airliner. It is bigger, heavier, and can carry more people than the largest Boeing 747. It is also the first jet airliner to have two full-length passenger decks. The A380 has been designed for efficiency. Refueling between flights takes ninety minutes or less.

Airbus is a European company whose first airliner was the A300,

The Airbus A380 has two complete decks. It carries more passengers than any other airliner in service today.

which first flew in 1972. The main parts of the A380 are made in factories in Britain, Germany, Spain, and other countries. The airplanes are assembled in France.

At first, Airbus called its new design the A3XX, but renamed it the A380. The first A380 flew on April 27, 2005. Emirates, Qantas,

A380 CABIN LAYOUTS
The A380 can carry a large number of passengers on its upper and lower decks.
It also has an increased cargo capacity.

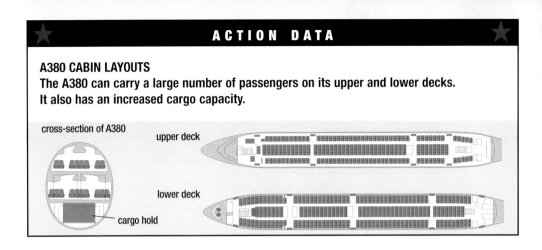

cross-section of A380   upper deck

lower deck

cargo hold

Virgin, and ANA airlines have all ordered at least one Airbus 380.

800 Passengers or More

The first model of A380 can carry 555 passengers, with a mix of economy, business, and first-class seats. Airlines can also choose a single-class layout for as many as eight hundred passengers. Later models may carry even more.

Some airlines plan to include lounges, bars, and fitness centers in place of some seats.

Only certain airports with wide **taxiways** and special passenger bridges for on- and off-loading can accommodate such large aircraft. Airport owners all around the world are spending millions of dollars equipping their airports for the A380.

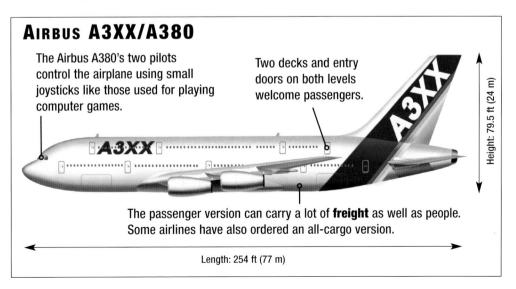

AIRBUS **A3XX/A380**

The Airbus A380's two pilots control the airplane using small joysticks like those used for playing computer games.

Two decks and entry doors on both levels welcome passengers.

Height: 79.5 ft (24 m)

The passenger version can carry a lot of **freight** as well as people. Some airlines have also ordered an all-cargo version.

Length: 254 ft (77 m)

Glossary

altimeter — an instrument for measuring the height at which an airplane flies

altitude — the height of a plane, or other object, above land or water

biplane — an airplane with two sets of wings, located one above the other

canard — a horizontal flying surface mounted in front of the wing to control the direction of the aircraft

canopy — the transparent covering over the cockpit

cockpit — the place where the flight crew sits to control the aircraft

compresses — squeezes together, often with increasing pressure

converted — changed into another form

data — information, such as specific facts and measurements

delta wing — a wing that looks like a triangle when seen from above

drag — a force that slows down an aircraft

epic — a task or action that is unusual, difficult, and lasts a long time

fin — the fixed part of an airplane's vertical (upright) tail

fairings — parts of the body of an airplane intended to reduce drag

foreplanes — small wings at the front of an airplane

four-cylinder piston engine — an engine that creates power when burning fuel explodes inside four round holes, forcing the pistons to move up and down

freight — goods carried by airplanes, ships, or other vehicles

fuselage — the main body of an airplane

headwind — a wind blowing directly against the direction of a vehicle

investors — people who provide money for a project in hopes of making money

monoplane — an airplane with a single set of wings

Mach 1 — a high speed, often used to describe the speed of sound in air

NASA — National Aeronautics and Space Administration

prototype — an original model, often made for testing a design

retractable — able to be drawn back inside

radial engine — engine with cylinders arranged like the spokes of a wheel

rudder — control at the rear (aft) of a craft that helps it turn

seaplanes — airplanes that take off and land from water

sonic boom — a very loud bang caused when an airplane flies faster than the speed of sound

skid — a support that enables heavy objects to be moved by sliding

solo — unaccompanied; working alone

stratosphere — the part of the Earth's atmosphere that extends from 7 miles (11 km) to 31 miles (50 km) above Earth's surface

supersonic — faster than the speed of sound

tailplane — the horizontal (flat) part of an airplane's tail

taxiways — roadlike, paved areas at airports that lead to the runways

turbofan — a jet engine with a large fan at the front

undercarriage — the legs and the wheels, skis, or skids that an airplane lands on

For More Information

Books

Amelia Earhart. Trailblazers of the Modern World (series). Lucia Raatma (World Almanac® Library)

Charles Lindbergh. Famous Flyers (series). Heather Lehr Wagner (Facts on File)

Chuck Yeager. Famous Flyers (series). Colleen Madonna Flood Williams (Facts on File)

First Flight: The Story of Tom Tate and the Wright Brothers. I Can Read Chapter Book (series). George Shea (HarperCollins Children's Books)

The Glorious Flight: Across the Channel with Louis Bleriot, July 25, 1909. Alice Provensen and Martin Provensen (Puffin)

Web sites

Guinness World Records — Aircraft
Includes facts and statistics on record-breaking aircraft.
*www.guinnessworldrecords.com/content_pages/record_subcategory.
asp?subcategoryid=66*

The Official Amelia Earhart site
Offers a comprehensive history of Amelia Earhart's life and achievements.
www.ameliaearhart.com/

Science Museum, London — Louis Blériot
A site that outlines the history of Louis Bleriot's record breaking flight, with links to other facts about the history of flight.
www.sciencemuseum.org.uk/on-line/flight/flight/bleriot.asp

U.S. Centennial of Flight Commission — Kid's Fly Zone
This celebrates the people, events, and science that made flight possible.
www.centennialofflight.gov/user/kids.htm

Publisher's note to educators and parents: Our editors have carefully reviewed these Web sites to ensure that they are suitable for children. Many Web sites change frequently, however, and we cannot guarantee that a site's future contents will continue to meet our high standards of quality and educational value. Be advised that children should be closely supervised whenever they access the Internet.

Index